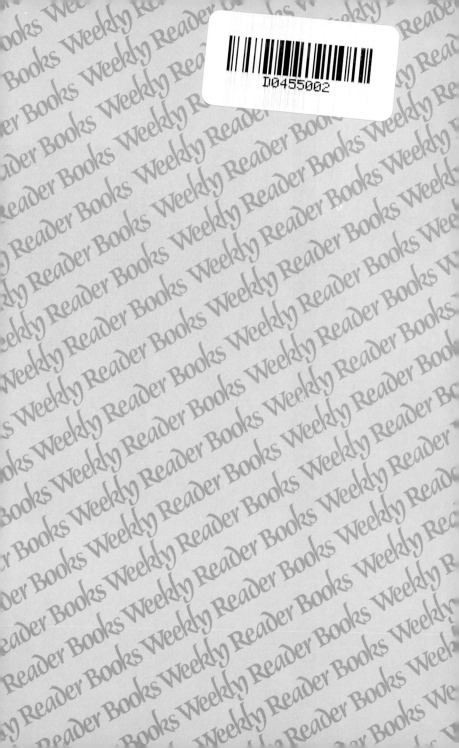

Dear Reader,

Imagine being able to make a boring teacher disappear. Just close your eyes and wish the teacher away.

If that sounds interesting, then you'll love reading *Mr. Radagast Makes an Unexpected Journey.* That's because a bunch of students like you actually make their teacher disappear.

Here's what happens: Mr. Radagast tries to demonstrate the "theory of immaterialism" (an actual theory) with a classroom experiment. Only the experiment backfires and Mr. Radagast . . .

Actually, I don't want to spoil it for you. To find out what happens, just start reading.

Sincerely,

Elizabeth Isele
Executive Editor
Weekly Reader Books

Weekly Reader Books Presents

Mr. Radagast Makes an Unexpected Journey

Sharon Nastick

Illustrated by Judy Glasser

Thomas Y. Crowell   New York

Text copyright © 1981 by Sharon Nastick
Illustrations copyright © 1981 by Judy Glasser
All rights reserved. Printed in the United States of America. No part of this book may be used or reproduced in any manner whatsoever without written permission except in the case of brief quotations embodied in critical articles and reviews. For information address Thomas Y. Crowell Junior Books, 10 East 53rd Street, New York, N.Y. 10022. Published simultaneously in Canada by Fitzhenry & Whiteside Limited, Toronto.
Designed by Harriett Barton

Library of Congress Cataloging in Publication Data
Nastick, Sharon.
Mr. Radagast makes an unexpected journey.
SUMMARY: While trying to prove the scientific theory that objects can be willed to disappear, a seventh-grade class comes up with some unexpected results.
    [1.   School stories]   I.   Glasser, Judy.   II.   Title.
PZ7.M1739Mi   1981   [Fic]   80–8017
ISBN 0–690–04050–4   ISBN 0–690–04051–2 (lib. bdg.)

For my parents,
my family,
and all of
Mr. Radagast's
friends

Contents

Mr. Radagast
Makes an
Unexpected
Journey

1
The
Experiment

Mr. Radagast smiled at his class, displaying his teeth in their straight, even, shining rows. It was inconceivable that Mr. Radagast's teeth could be anything but straight, even, and shining. Every one of his almost seventy-two inches, from his plastered black hair to the matching bows of his shoelaces, was straight, even, and shining. When he spoke, his voice was a perfectly tuned monotone, and his words were tight and clear.

"Good afternoon, class. Today, in these first five minutes, I would like to tell you about a most intriguing theory."

In the ruler-straight rows of desks and chairs, the seventh graders fidgeted. A few yawned. The privileged six next to the windows gazed out at a pleasant October day. A playful northern breeze stirred the red and yellow leaves on the playground trees. There was a touch of dullness in the blue sky, but it was far surpassed by the dullness that perpetually hung over Mr. Radagast's classroom.

"The theory, as I know it, is called 'immaterialism.' It was developed by Bishop Berkeley, who lived in the eighteenth century, and it concerns the nature of reality."

Most of the children assumed their favorite

positions: hands on desk, chin on hands, eyes half-closed; or elbows on desk, head in hands, eyes half-closed. They knew what was coming. Mr. Radagast collected theories like Louella Pierson collected stamps. Whatever he talked about immediately sounded dusty and dreary, whether it was Einstein's ideas about relativity or Sagan's ideas about black holes in space. They had no reason to think that Berkeley's views on reality would be any different.

The only people paying any sort of attention were the Brains, the ones who listened to any adult who happened to speak. They were sitting up straight, notebooks open, ball-point pens in hand. "Immaterialism," they wrote carefully. "Bishop Berkeley."

"Berkeley believed," Mr. Radagast contin-ued, with chalk-free hands clasped behind his back, "that objects of themselves have no existence, that time and space and *everything* exist only as creations of our minds. In other words, this desk, this blackboard, this room exist only because we all *believe* that they exist."

Mr. Radagast paused to dwell on the wonder of what he had said. Four students fell asleep.

"Now it follows, I believe—and I have reasoned this with utmost care—that if we each had our own conceptions of space and time, and if we believed in them strongly enough, each of those different conceptions would be real and true. We could *make* them true. There could be a separate reality for each of us."

Still no one but the Brains was paying much attention. No one but the Brains, that is, and one boy, the boy who sat in the front seat of the window row. His name was Conrad McDermont. He was a tall, scrawny boy with wavy black hair and hazel eyes. Normally, he doodled and dozed his way through Mr. Radagast's lectures. But now he was wide awake. For the first time in that class, he had heard something interesting. He wanted to hear more. He raised his hand.

"You mean, you can just *think* something into existence?"

Mr. Radagast looked lost in his thoughts, but his voice conveyed his excitement. "That is theoretically correct. But no one has ever made it happen—"

"Then, can you think something *out* of existence too?"

"That logically follows."

"Have you ever done it?"

"Well—no." Mr. Radagast finally realized that a student had been asking him questions. The novelty of the situation surprised him so much that he forgot what he'd been asked. "Done what?"

"Thought something out of existence." Conrad felt the baleful glare of his classmates upon him. He was disturbing their afternoon nap.

"No. I've never done it. I mean, I've never *tried* it. I've been so busy trying to think things *into* existence, I have never considered thinking them *out*. But it should be possible. In fact, it might be *easier* to have something in front of you, some *thing* to work with, instead of some image in your—mind."

Mr. Radagast suddenly realized that his students were all staring at him as though he'd sprouted orange warts and an extra pair of ears. He cleared his throat and reminded himself that he was addressing children. They couldn't grasp theories without some sort of visual aid.

"Let me carry this idea a little further. Let us take my desk as an example. Suppose we were all to concentrate on this desk and say over and over to ourselves that it does not exist.

If the theory works, it will cease to exist."

"What will happen to it?" Conrad asked.

Mr. Radagast shook his head. "I don't know," he said slowly. "Perhaps it would simply—dissolve and not be anymore. Or maybe— it would go somewhere else."

"Like where?" Conrad knew he should have stopped right there, but his curiosity overcame his sense of social prerogative. "Where would it go if we made it cease to exist?"

Mr. Radagast shook his head again. "I don't know. As I said, I've never done it. As far as I know, no one's ever done it."

"Let's try to do it."

Groans filled the classroom, twenty-eight groans from twenty-eight throats. Only Mr. Radagast, Conrad, and one other did not groan. This other sat in the back seat in the row farthest away from the windows. He was a little shorter than Conrad, with blond hair and sharp gray eyes, and his name was Damon Kilpatrick. He normally spent his time in Mr. Radagast's class working on his spitballs. Damon made the best spitballs in the Mayfair Public School System. They were as round and hard as peashooter pellets; and when properly placed on the tongue, aimed, and fired, they traveled the distance from launch point to target with incredible speed and accuracy. Making such spitballs took a lot of time and work. Luckily for Damon, he had a lot of classes like this one where he could work without fear of distraction. But now, he swept his latest batch into his binder and looked at Mr. Radagast with an evil sparkle in his eyes.

"Why, yes!" Mr. Radagast said eagerly. He couldn't believe his good fortune. Not only was a student paying attention and asking questions, he actually wanted to take part in an experiment. "Yes, let's try it. We will need the cooperation of the entire class. I am sure that we will get it." Obviously, he was so excited that he was forgetting about his previous experiences in provoking class cooperation. "To begin, let us concentrate on my desk. Let us say over and over in our minds, 'Desk, you do not exist. Desk, you do not exist.' Let us begin now and continue for a full minute, with full concentration, and see what happens."

Mr. Radagast turned to face his desk and stared at it so hard that his eyes almost popped out of his head. Conrad stared at it. Damon stared at it. A few of the Brains, and one or two others, stared at it too. But full class cooperation was not in evidence. After sixty complete seconds, the desk still sat in the left corner of the classroom, as solid and real as ever.

"It doesn't work," someone snorted from the middle of the room.

"Dear, dear," Mr. Radagast said mournfully. "It never has."

"Let's try something else," Conrad suggested. "Let's try something smaller."

"What would you suggest, Conrad?"

"Umm—the science book!"

"A very good idea!" Mr. Radagast carefully balanced the thick textbook on the exact middle of his desk. "Now, class, let us concentrate again. 'Book, you do not exist. Book, you do not exist.' "

There was a bit more concentration this time. The students, in general, wished to be left in peace. Perceiving that this would not happen until Mr. Radagast was satisfied, they stared at the book as hard as they could.

Sixty seconds later, the book was still in

place. But Conrad had noticed something.

"It wavered! It got kind of blurry around the edges, just for a second or two!"

"Did it? I didn't notice!" The teacher snatched the book from his desk and clapped it to his chest. "Class, we may be on the verge of a scientific breakthrough—proof of Berkeley's theory! Concentrate harder! *Make* this book cease to exist!"

Thirty bodies hunched forward out of their seats. Sixty eyes stared at the front of the room. Thirty minds all thought the same thought.

But they weren't thinking about the book.

Mr. Radagast's jaw danced with excitement. His perfect teeth trembled. His eyes were glazed with anticipation, dreams of future glory. He didn't notice the hostility on their faces. He even forgot to concentrate on the book. And that, perhaps, was his fatal mistake.

One moment, Mr. Radagast, most unpopular teacher in Mayfair Junior High, was standing in front of his fourth-period class.

The next moment, he was gone.

The textbook hit the floor with a thud.

Thirty mouths fell open. Thirty bodies thumped back against their chairs.

There was silence—silence for a long, long time.

2
The
Problem

As usual, Damon broke the silence. His long, low whistle brought his friends back to life.

"We did it!"

"We really did it!"

"No more Radagast!"

"Hooray!"

Shouts and cheers and laughter swiftly filled the little room. The long-suffering students

14

stamped their feet, clapped their hands, and danced upon their desks and chairs, rejoicing in their sudden and wonderful liberation. Even the Brains joined in.

But Conrad still sat very, very still.

He stared at the empty space that had been full of Mr. Radagast scarcely five minutes ago.

What had they done?

Where had he gone?

Could they bring him back?

"We've *got* to bring him back!"

Conrad didn't realize he had spoken aloud until he noticed everyone staring at him.

"Are you *crazy?*" Damon demanded. "We've been dreaming of getting rid of him since school started. We've wished and hoped and prayed for this day. And now that we've finally done it, you want to bring him *back?*"

"We've *got* to bring him back!" Conrad

snapped, his anger rising to match Damon's outrage.

"Why?"

"Because people are going to wonder what happened to him. He's not married, but his parents and his sisters live right here in Mayfair. If he doesn't show up in a couple of days— maybe even a couple of hours—people are going to start asking questions. It won't take them too long to figure out that we might have been the last people to see him. The police will come for us. And when they do—"

"We'll tell them the truth," Louella Pierson suggested. She was one of the Brains and usually smarter than that.

Conrad shook his head. "They won't believe us. They'll think we're lying. They might even think that we—killed him."

The mighty gasp from twenty-nine throats shook the fluorescent lights on the ceiling.

"So," Conrad concluded, "we've *got* to bring him back."

"How?" Damon wanted to know.

"If we can think him away," Conrad said, "we can think him back again."

"That's logical," Louella agreed. "Mr. Radagast *said* it should work both ways."

"Let's try it. Back to your seats, everyone."

All twenty-nine students sat down again.

"When I say 'Go,' " said Conrad, "we'll all stare at the front of the room and concentrate on bringing Mr. Radagast back from wherever he is. Ready? Go!"

They sat as they had before, leaning forward and staring at the exact place where Mr. Radagast had last been seen.

Sixty seconds passed.

Sixty more seconds passed.

At the end of three minutes, Conrad gave up.

"It's no good," he said. "We can't do it."

"Logically," Louella frowned, "we should be able to do it."

"I know what's wrong!" Damon jumped out of his seat. "We can think as long and hard as we can, but we still won't be able to do it, because we don't really *want* Mr. Radagast back."

No one could deny that truth.

"So what do we do now?" someone asked.

For the first time, all eyes turned to Louella without contempt. Even though she was a Brain, she might have a sensible answer. But she blushed and shook her head from side to side, just as Mr. Radagast had.

Conrad knew what had to be done. His spine shivered at the thought, but he forced himself to stand straight and tall, to look courageous even though he didn't feel that way. "You'll have to make me cease to exist so I can find him."

The classroom was so quiet that Conrad could hear the lunch boxes creaking in the closet.

"I have an objection." The crease on Louella's forehead sunk a little deeper. "If we can't think Mr. Radagast back, how do we know that he *did* go somewhere? How can we be sure that he isn't just—gone?"

"We can't be sure," Conrad admitted. "We don't know. But I'm going to find out."

"But if we can't get Mr. Radagast back, how do we know that we can get you back?"

"You'll be able to, all right," Damon said confidently. "Not all of you wanted Mr. Radagast back, but you all *will* want Conrad and me to come back, won't you?"

"Sure!" everyone said.

"So when you think us back, it won't be so

hard to think Mr. Radagast back. Right?"

"Right!"

"Hold it!" Conrad turned to face Damon. "Who said you were coming with me?"

"You don't want to go alone, do you?" Damon's earnestly innocent expression didn't agree with the mischief in his eyes.

"It's dangerous. We might not come back. Why should both of us risk it?"

"Two heads are better than one."

"He might be right," Louella said.

"Maybe you can't think three of us back at the same time."

"It might be easier."

Conrad tried to think of another good reason why Damon shouldn't come. Was not liking the obnoxious creep good enough? Probably not. Besides, it was too late. Damon was already heading for the front of the room, his jeans pockets bulging with spitballs, a sly smirk on his face that suggested Conrad had better not give him any trouble. Damon was smaller than Conrad; but he was also tougher than Conrad, and both boys knew it.

"Should we stand where Mr. Radagast stood?" he asked.

"Yes, that'll be best."

As their friends prepared to repeat the experiment, Damon and Conrad took their places at the front of the room, right behind the science book.

"Are you sure you want to do this?" Conrad asked him, in a low voice so the rest of the class wouldn't hear.

"I'm sure," Damon said in the same soft tone.

"Why?"

"I'll tell you when we get there."

Damon looked too calm for someone who was about to cease to exist. Did he know something Conrad didn't? Or was he too dumb to realize

what could happen to them? Well, if he wanted
to come along, he could. It was his decision.
His life.

Together they faced their friends for what
they knew was possibly the last time.

Conrad looked at Louella. "How long until
the end of the period?"

Louella glanced at her wristwatch. "About
forty minutes."

"All right. In about thirty-five minutes, start
thinking us back. If we haven't found Mr. Radagast by then—we'll have to try again tomorrow.
Ready, Damon?"

"Ready, Conrad." Damon slapped his loaded
pockets with both hands.

"All right," Conrad said, not as confident
as Damon seemed to be. "Look at us and start
thinking, start concentrating, just like you did
for Mr. Radagast. 'They do not exist. They do
not exist. They do not exist—' "

3
Saved
by a
Spitball

Conrad tried to keep his eyes wide open. Whatever happened, he wanted to see it. But when
the faces of his friends blurred and the classroom rocked, he had to close his eyes for a
second, just to steady himself.

All at once he tingled with the heady sensation of being suspended in time and space, with
no roof over his head and no floor under his
feet.

24

When he felt ground again, he opened his eyes.

Quickly he made sure that Damon was at his side.

The smaller boy's face was pale, but he smiled when he saw Conrad.

"Well—here we are."

Conrad grinned. "I guess we didn't 'cease to exist' after all."

They turned their eyes to what lay in front of them.

What lay in front of them was—nothing.

Nothing but gray, shapeless blankness.

"Or did we?" Damon's grin wavered around the edges.

"I don't know." Conrad made his voice stay calm. He was as scared as Damon, but he wasn't about to show it. "This isn't what I thought it would be."

"What did you think it would be?"

"I don't know. *Something*. But this is *nothing*."

Cautiously, carefully, the two boys looked around them. Gray surrounded them on all sides, over their heads, and under their feet. Conrad felt cold and clammy all over. He wished he'd brought his sweater.

"Do you see Mr. Radagast?"

"Are you kidding?" Damon asked, with some of his old snide spirit. "Mr. Radagast could be standing three inches away and we couldn't see him through this stuff."

"But he might hear us." Conrad cupped his hands around his mouth. "Mr. Radagast! Mr. Radagast!"

Damon followed his example. "Mr. Rada*gast!* Mr. Rada*gast!*"

They called from side to side, behind them, and before them, and paused in between yells to listen for an answer.

None came.

"Now what?" Damon asked.

"We're going to have to look for him."

"You mean—move?"

"That's the idea."

"But how do we know there's any place to move *to?*" Damon had gone pale again, so pale he practically glowed against the gray. "How do we know Mr. Radagast didn't just step off this place we're standing on and drop out of sight?"

"You'd think a spitball maker would have more courage."

Angry color flooded Damon's cheeks. "You calling me a coward?"

"Yeah, I'm calling you a coward. In *this* world, anyway."

"*Forget* about following you! *You* follow *me!*"

And Damon took a giant step forward.

Conrad half expected him to vanish.

But Damon was still there. He looked back at Conrad and grinned. "Who's a coward now?"

Conrad stepped next to him.

For a few moments they walked in silence, close together. Conrad was sure that if they walked long enough, they would come out of the gray and see where they were. If only they could *see* something! If only they could *hear* something! The silence was almost as bad as the grayness. When Damon murmured under his breath, Conrad heard every word as clearly as though he'd shouted into his ear.

"We'd better find him, that's all. If we came here for nothing—"

"How come you came along? You said you'd tell me."

"Simple." Damon kept his eyes straight

ahead. "Mr. Radagast is in trouble. He's alone and scared and probably desperate. When he sees that we've come to rescue him, he'll be so grateful that he'll give us anything we want."

"What are you going to ask him for?"

"Not much." Damon took a crisp fresh spitball out of his pocket and flipped it into the air, just like a gangster tossing a coin in an old movie. "Just straight A's for the rest of the semester and help with my project for the science fair."

"You're going to make him pay for his own rescue? When it's our fault he's here?"

"Sure," Damon said matter-of-factly. "It's bad enough we've got to bring him back. The least he can do is a little favor."

"Well, *I'm* not going to ask for anything. I just want to get him back, safe and sound."

"Figures."

"What's *that* supposed to mean?"

"You're such a holy hero you'd never think of doing anything for yourself."

"You're jealous. You wish you were like me, noble and unselfish—"

"And *dumb!*" Damon's laughter cut through the gray like a sword through cream cheese.

Conrad glared at him. Noble he might be, but at that moment he would have loved to sock Damon in the jaw and really rattle his molars.

Damon staggered back, clasping his face with both hands.

"Oww!"

"Damon! What's wrong?"

"I don't know! I feel like someone just slugged me!"

"I didn't touch you!"

"I *know* you didn't." Damon clutched his cheeks.

"Are you okay?" Conrad came close to him.

"I think so. But my back teeth feel funny. They're vibrating like they do when I use my electric toothbrush."

"Hold still."

"Why?"

"Just hold still a minute."

Conrad thought about making Damon's teeth be still.

Damon let go of his face.

"Are you okay now?"

"Yeah. I feel fine. The tingling stopped. How did you do that?"

"I thought about it."

"And?"

"That's all. I just thought about it."

"I don't get it." Damon looked puzzled.

"I think I do. Let me think about something else."

Conrad's throat was dry from calling Mr.

Radagast's name over and over. He thought of a sparkling crystal glass filled with cold, fresh, pure water. He held out his hand to hold it.

It was there.

Damon whistled. "That's some trick! But is it real?"

Conrad tasted the water. Just one sip wiped out his thirst and made him feel cool all over.

"It's real. It's delicious. It's *perfect!*"

"Let *me* try some!" Damon rudely snatched the glass out of Conrad's hand and gulped down the rest of the water. He licked his lips and rolled his eyes. "I've never tasted water like that before, but it's real, all right! Thanks, Conrad."

Conrad took the glass back.

"Can you make it disappear?"

Conrad thought of the glass not being there.

He tried to imagine it disappearing, going back to wherever it had come from.

The glass remained in his hand.

"No. I can't"

"How'd you get it there in the first place?" Damon looked awed.

"Just by thinking about it." Conrad put the glass down on the gray under his feet. "Just like Mr. Radagast said—reality is what we think it is. *Here* we can think up our own realities and make them happen."

"Let me try." Damon spread his legs wide apart. He clasped his hands behind his back. He stared straight ahead.

Just watching him made Conrad queasy. What was he up to? What was he thinking about? What was he making in his mind?

"Damon—"

"Shh!" the spitball maker hissed between

tightly clenched teeth. Conrad didn't bother him again.

For several seconds, nothing happened. Maybe Damon couldn't do it. Maybe he, Conrad, was the only one who could do it. He liked that thought. If Damon gave him any more trouble, all he had to do was think about stepping on his feet or boxing his ears and it would be done. He wouldn't have to lift a finger or scrape his knuckles.

Green glowed in the gray.

Conrad caught his breath.

About five hundred yards ahead of them, a thing was taking shape.

It was fifty feet tall, give or take a few feet. It had long hind legs with big feet, short forelegs, long claws, a massive head, mighty jaws, and mean little eyes.

"Wha—wha—" Conrad had to take a deep

breath before he could finally say, "What is it?"

"It's a Tyrannosaurus Rex," Damon whispered. "A dinosaur! Shh! You'll scare it."

That sounded fair enough to Conrad. *It* was scaring *him.* "What did you think of *that* for?"

"I wanted to see what it looked like."

"Is it alive?"

To answer his question, the Tyrannosaurus growled like thunder and moved its head from side to side.

"It's alive!" Damon gasped gleefully, just like a mad scientist.

"Will it hurt us?"

"It won't get a chance." Damon picked a spitball out of his pocket.

"What are you going to do with that?"

"Kill it, when it attacks us."

"With a *spitball?*" If the dinosaur hadn't been so close, Conrad would have laughed.

"If I think, I can."

The Tyrannosaurus stepped in their direction.

Damon poised the spitball on the tip of his tongue.

"Maybe it won't hurt us."

"Better safe than sorry," Damon said barely moving his tongue.

The Tyrannosaurus moved faster, lifting its tail off the ground. Conrad could see its teeth— long, sharp, and stained with blood.

"Damon!"

Damon fired.

The spitball struck the dinosaur squarely on the chest.

The Tyrannosaurus threw back its head and roared louder than a lion.

Damon fired again.

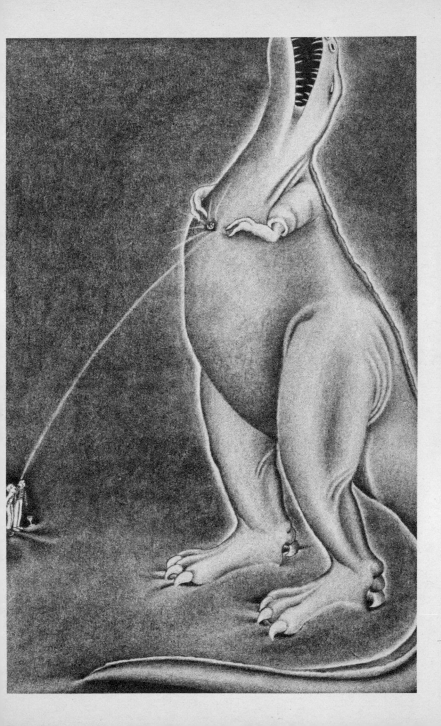

The clawed forelegs scratched at the stricken chest.

The great beast crashed to the ground, shuddered, then lay quite still.

4
Good
Thinking

For a few moments, the two boys were as still
as the dinosaur.

"You killed it," Conrad said at last.

"It would have killed us," Damon replied,
almost in apology.

"You don't know that."

"T-Rexes are meat eaters."

"You should have thought of that before

you thought him into existence. You saw how we couldn't get rid of the glass. If only your brain was as big as your mouth."

Too late, Conrad remembered that no one ever insulted Damon Kilpatrick and remained unbloodied. Damon glared through narrowed eyes. "I ought to think that dinosaur back to life and—"

An unholy glitter lit his gaze. Without another word, he swung to face the dinosaur. He stood straight, hands clasped behind his back.

"Damon?"

His eyes were riveted to the dead reptile.

"Damon! Don't!"

Sweat beaded Damon's forehead, which was furrowed deeper than Louella's on a test day.

Helplessly, Conrad looked at the Tyrannosaurus.

Its little eyes opened wide.

It rolled to its feet, towering over the two boys. It glared at them, but did not move.

Conrad tried to speak, to beg Damon for mercy, before he thought his awful plan into action. But only a dry gasp came through his lips.

The Tyrannosaurus threw back its massive head and roared once more, shaking both boys from head to toe.

Then it turned its back on them and lumbered away.

Conrad stared at the dinosaur's broad back until it vanished in the gray. Then his voice came back.

"You revived it, Damon. Congratulations."

"Almost killed me to do it." His voice was shaky. "That was harder than thinking him up in the first place. I've never thought so hard in my life. My head hurts. I think I broke my brain." All of a sudden, Damon sat down, although there was nothing to sit *on*. He cradled his head between his knees.

Conrad sat down with him and pushed his glass to one side. He thought of thanking Damon for saving his life, but decided against it. He didn't want to inspire him to think up another monstrous scheme.

"Well, we have proven two things." Conrad felt as smart as a college professor. "In *our* world, we can concentrate on someone—or something—and make it cease to exist. In *this* world, we can concentrate on someone—or something—and make it exist."

"Yeah." Damon lifted his head. "Anything we want?"

"I guess so."

"Money? Ice cream? Bicycles?"

"Yeah!" Suddenly, Conrad remembered the ten-speed racing bike he had wanted for his birthday. His dad had said it was too expensive. A few moments of hard thinking and it would be his for free.

Damon shook his head. He winced. "You go right ahead and think. My head still hurts."

"Think your pain away. Or think up a clear head to replace your headache—whatever you have to do."

"It hurts worse when I think about it." Damon hid his head between his legs again. "Why don't you think about Mr. Radagast so we can get out of here?"

Mr. Radagast! Conrad had totally forgotten about Mr. Radagast.

"Damon, do you have a watch?"

"No."

"How long do you think we've been here?"

"Maybe fifteen minutes."

"Clear your head fast so we can think about Mr. Radagast."

"*You* do it."

"It might be faster if we both do it."

"Then shut up for a minute!" Damon covered his ears with his knees.

Conrad leaned back on his hands. The bicycle would have to wait. Mr. Radagast was more important. At least his parents and sisters would think so.

In exactly sixty seconds, Damon's head bobbed up. He grinned at Conrad with an unfurrowed brow. "Ready to think?"

"Ready."

The two boys got to their feet. Automatically, Conrad brushed off the seat of his jeans, though no gray stuff stuck to them.

"Why do you stand like that?" he asked Damon as the other boy took a stalwart stance.

"Helps me to think better."

"I never see you stand that way in school."

"Who thinks in school?"

Conrad declined to discuss the question. "Let's both look straight ahead, at the same point, and think of Mr. Radagast as we last saw him."

"With or without the science book?"

"With."

"But he didn't take it with him."

"But it'll be harder to think of him without it. Look, if we don't think exactly alike, we might not get him."

"Okay."

"On three. One—two—three."

Conrad brought Mr. Radagast into his mind, top to toe. He remembered the excited expression on his face, the thick textbook trembling in his hands. He remembered the color of his suit, the shine of his teeth, the bristly hairs at the edges of his mustache, the bobbing Adam's apple in his throat.

And the image began to form, not more than twenty feet away.

Three seconds later, there stood Mr. Radagast, perfect in every detail, even to the frayed binding of the science book.

"Mr. Radagast!" Conrad cried.

"Mr. Radagast!" Damon called.

"Good afternoon, Conrad," Mr. Radagast said, smiling serenely.

"Damon! Damon, my *dear, clever, brilliant* boy! How glad I am to see you!"

That was Mr. Radagast's voice again. But Mr. Radagast's lips hadn't moved. *He* hadn't spoken those frantic words.

Who had?

When Conrad looked to his right, he found the answer.

He found another Mr. Radagast.

5
Teacher, Twice

The second Mr. Radagast was not as calm and composed as the first. His hair waved wildly around his head like black grass in a high wind. His torn pants fluttered over legs cut and bruised, and his tie was gone. He crawled to Damon on hands and knees, like a big baby. Damon just stood there, his hands crossed over his chest, and watched him. His grin had turned into a nasty smirk.

"Damon! What did you do?" Amazement and anger fought for control of Conrad's voice.

"I thought of Mr. Radagast the way I've always wanted to see him."

"That's not what I told you to do."

"That's what I *wanted* to do."

Conrad looked at his own Mr. Radagast. He stood in his place, wearing the same silly smile, clutching the science book to his well-dressed chest.

"Mr. Radagast," he called. "Would you wait there, please?"

"Of course, Conrad. I'll be here if you need me."

Could he see his twin? Did it embarrass him to see himself groveling on the ground before Damon? If it did, he didn't show it. Either he was pretending not to notice or he *didn't* notice. Maybe Mr. Radagast really was nearsighted, as some people said, but too vain to wear glasses, though he had no excuse for vanity.

The second Mr. Radagast embraced Damon's feet and rested his head on the boy's sneakered toes. "I've been *so* scared, *so* frightened! I thought I was going to die! I thought you'd never find me! But here you are! How can I *ever* repay you?"

"By giving me straight A's for the rest of the year and helping me with my science-fair project," the shameless student said.

"I will! I will!" Big, blubbery tears of joy rolled down the teacher's sunken cheeks.

Conrad had seen enough. "That's *not* the real Mr. Radagast!"

"Maybe not," Damon said, looking down at him with fiendish pleasure. "But I like him, and he's the one I'm taking home with me."

"Oh no you're not! You think him away right now!"

"Why should I?"

"Because I'm telling you to."

Damon's grin flattened into a dangerous frown. His gray eyes narrowed into sneaky slots. "That's not a good enough reason."

"You want a better one?"

"Yeah."

Conrad thought fast. "No one will ever believe that's the real Mr. Radagast. He'd never let himself get that dirty."

"They'll believe him if he says so. And he'll say so if I tell him to."

"And how will you explain *my* Mr. Radagast?"

"What Mr. Radagast?"

"There!" Conrad pointed to him.

Damon hadn't noticed the other man. Now he saw him. He whistled. "That's him, all right. Nice work. Is he alive?"

"Of course he's alive. Mr. Radagast! Come here!"

"Coming, Conrad." He walked slowly toward them, still holding the science book against his chest.

Damon shuddered. "He's creepy. Walks like a zombie. The *real* Mr. Radagast doesn't walk like that."

"This *is* the real Mr. Radagast. You said yourself that he was perfect."

"That was before he moved. Make him stop before he comes any closer!"

"Stop, Mr. Radagast. Please wait."

"All right, Conrad." He stopped on the spot.

"Let go of my feet, Mr. Radagast," Damon said. "You're getting my shoes all wet."

"Of course, *dear* Damon. Sorry. Sorry." The messy Mr. Radagast slid back on his belly like a cowardly snake.

"Go back to where you were before and wait for me there."

"All right, Damon." He slid back to his former place. He didn't look up at the other Mr. Radagast, and the other Mr. Radagast didn't look at him.

Conrad and Damon looked at each other.

"I don't think either of them is the real Mr. Radagast," Damon said at last.

"I think you're right," Conrad agreed. "I guess I couldn't help thinking of my own Mr. Radagast either."

"So which one do we take back with us?"

"Neither."

"*Neither?*"

"We've got to find the real one. An imitation won't do."

"Are you sure?" Damon asked wistfully, glancing at the grateful, squirming Mr. Radagast who would obey all commands.

"I'm sure," Conrad said, looking at the quiet, serene Mr. Radagast, who was equally obedient and almost as repulsive.

"So what do we do with these guys? We can think them up, but we can't think them away."

"Tell them to go away."

"You tell yours first."

Conrad cleared his throat. "Mr. Radagast, would you please walk away?"

"Certainly, Conrad. In which direction should I go?"

"To the right."

"Thank you. Good-bye." And he walked to the right, taking his sickly sweet smile with him.

"Get *out* of here, Mr. Radagast!" Damon

shouted. "Shoo! Scat! Don't come near me ever again!"

"Anything you say, Damon!"

The other Mr. Radagast crawled away like a beaten dog. Conrad couldn't look at him. Even though he wasn't the real Mr. Radagast, he hated to see him brought so low.

In a minute, both teachers were as lost as the dinosaur.

6
Finding Mr. Radagast

"So," Damon said, once they were alone, "what do we do now?"

"We concentrate on finding the real Mr. Radagast," Conrad said.

"How? We tried that already and all we got were fakes. How do we find the real one?"

Conrad hoped he knew the answer. "He's probably figured out how this place works, like we have, and he's probably expecting to spend the rest of his life here, so he's probably made himself a nice place to live."

"If it's something he's thought up, why can't we see it?"

"Maybe he doesn't *want* it to be seen."

"You mean he doesn't want to be found?"

"Could be."

"That's stupid. Who would want to live *here?*" Damon's hands waved through the unending gray.

"*That's* stupid. Wouldn't you rather live in a place where you could have anything you wanted just by thinking about it, instead of a place where people make fun of you and don't listen to you?"

"So how do we find him?" Damon had an irritating habit of repeating important questions until they were answered.

"We can't think about him," Conrad reasoned aloud, "because if we do, we'll just get his doubles again. And we can't think about where he is, because we don't know what kind of world he would make for himself. So what we have to do is—"

"What?" Damon asked after fifteen seconds of silence.

"I don't know yet."

"We don't have much time."

"I'm *thinking!*"

"Why don't you think about thinking up how we're going to think Mr. Radagast back?"

"If you say 'think' one more time, I'm going to think you clear to—" Conrad's brain jumped against his skull. "Damon! That's it!"

"That's what?"

"Instead of thinking Mr. Radagast to *us*, let's think *us* to *him!*"

"Huh?" For someone who had just inspired a brilliant idea, Damon had a stupid expression on his face.

"All we have to do is clear our minds, leave them totally open, and think about where Mr. Radagast is. Don't picture him. Don't picture *anything*. Just make your mind absolutely blank and let Mr. Radagast's dream world fill it up."

"I don't get it," Damon frowned, his hands deep in his spitball-lined pockets.

"I don't know if I can explain it any better. Yes I can! It's like looking at a blank TV screen in your head. Don't turn on the TV. Just think over and over, 'Show me where Mr. Radagast is.' But don't *imagine* where he is."

"I think I get it." Damon still frowned. "But I don't know if it'll work."

"I don't either. It's worth a try, though."

"But you understand it better than I do.

Maybe *you* can make it work, but I don't know if *I* can."

"Just do your best." Conrad knew what Damon was worried about. "Hang on to me, and maybe we won't be separated."

"Mr. Radagast and his book got separated."

"The book couldn't think. You can. Right?"

To Conrad's relief, Damon's gloom gave way to a grin. "Want to see another dinosaur?"

"No thanks. One's enough for me."

The two boys moved close together, shoulder to shoulder, hip to hip, knee to knee, left foot to right foot.

"Ready?"

"Ready."

"Prepare to blank out. Close your eyes, and one—two—three."

Conrad emptied his head. He let go of everything but one strong thought: Show me where Mr. Radagast is.

In a few moments, he saw a long red building, like a giant brick, with no windows or doors— at least that he could see.

Take us there, Conrad thought.

Something scraped his nose. He opened his eyes. Red brick stared at him.

Conrad stepped back, rubbing his nose. He hadn't planned to come *this* close.

"He's in here?" Damon was rubbing his nose too. Conrad was glad he had made it.

"Isn't this what you saw?"

"Yeah, at first. Then I thought I saw a classroom, but before I could really focus, I was up against the wall."

"A classroom? You think this is a school?"

"Could be," Damon shrugged. "What else would a teacher think of?"

"Let's find a way in."

The two boys followed the brick wall for almost half a mile before they turned the corner and found a tall wooden door with a curved iron handle.

Before they opened it, Conrad put his ear against the wood to see if he could hear anything.

The familiar rise and fall of Mr. Radagast's voice droned through the heavy door.

"He's in there," Conrad confirmed.

"Is he in trouble?" Damon reached for a spitball.

"I don't think so. Sounds like he's giving a lecture."

"We'd better go in and get him before the class turns on him."

"We'd better watch out. He may have thought up some friends."

"Do we charge in and take him by surprise, or sneak in and check out the situation first?"

"I'm in favor of sneaking."

"Fine with me. Here." Damon pressed ten spitballs into Conrad's hand. "Just in case they aren't friendly," he explained.

"Thanks."

Conrad clutched the spitballs in his left hand. With the right, he wrapped his fingers around the cold handle and pushed the door with his shoulder.

Damon squeezed in as soon as he could.

Conrad came right behind him.

7
The
Perfect
Classroom

The classroom was as big as a football field and packed to the walls with desks, chairs, and people of all ages and sizes. Each person had a notebook on his desk, a pen in his hand, and his eyes magnetically fixed on the man behind the podium in the front of the room, straight across from Conrad and Damon.

Outwardly, Mr. Radagast hadn't changed a

bit. He wore the pressed suit, the plastered hair, the trimmed mustache, and the thin tie. But his stern frown, his lowering eyebrows, and the piercing stare he gave the intruders were strange and new.

Conrad and Damon stood in the door, not sure of what to do. Did Mr. Radagast recognize them? Would he order them out? Would he make them sit down and listen to his lecture?

"Who *dares,*" the teacher rumbled in a voice quite unlike the one they knew, "to interrupt the Great Radagast in so rude and crude a fashion? Identify yourselves!"

Conrad took a brave step forward. "We are Conrad McDermont and Damon Kilpatrick, from Mayfair Junior High School. May we speak to you, please, Mr. Radagast?"

Mr. Radagast gripped the podium as though he feared they had come to take it away. His

mouth hung open so wide that Conrad could see his molars.

"Class dis—dismissed," Mr. Radagast whispered. Then he jerked himself to attention. "Class dismissed!"

The two boys dived away from the door as the hundreds of students stood up, picked up their notebooks, and filed out in perfect silence.

When the last student closed the door, Conrad and Damon ran to their teacher. The podium was shaking like a school bus. So was Mr. Radagast.

"Mr. Radagast! Are you all right?"

"I don't think so," he replied, in a voice as shaky as the rest of him. "I—I think I had better sit down."

Damon grabbed a chair and pushed it behind the teacher. Conrad helped Mr. Radagast to bend into it.

"Damon," he said, a little steadier, "inside

the podium you will find a pitcher of water and a glass. If you would be so kind—"

"Of course, sir," Damon said with a new— for him—tone of respect, and picked up the pitcher. Conrad stayed next to the trembling man.

"I'm sorry we scared you, Mr. Radagast. I guess we should have knocked or waited until the class was over. But we were so glad to see you—"

"That's all right, Conrad. Thank you, Damon."

He slowly drank the entire glass of water, sighed, placed the glass on the floor, and delicately wiped his lips with his spotless handkerchief. "Now then. How did you come here?"

"The same way you did," Conrad said. "We told the class to think us out of existence, and they did."

"And why have you come?"

"To take you back."

Mr. Radagast's eyes popped wide open. His hands, folded in his lap, suddenly trembled all over again. "Back? Back to Mayfair?"

"More water, sir?" Damon offered hastily.

"No. Back to Mayfair?"

"Yes, sir. The class is going to think us back at the end of the period."

"They—*you* want me back?"

"Of course we do," Damon said, looking guilty, which was also new for him.

"But I thought you couldn't stand the sight of me," Mr. Radagast said in amazement.

"Sure we can," Conrad said.

"We'll try to," Damon promised.

"Perhaps—" the teacher said doubtfully.

"Unless, of course, you'd rather stay here."

As Conrad glared and Mr. Radagast stared, Damon hastened to explain himself. "I mean, we can see that everything is perfect for you here. You've got students who listen to you, people who do what you say. What more could you want?"

"My *freedom!*" Mr. Radagast yelled, startling both his students. "My *freedom!*"

"But you can leave any time you want. Can't you?"

"No." Mr. Radagast slumped in his chair. "I've tried. I've been here for hours, *days* perhaps, a long time—however time is measured here—teaching and lecturing until I'm hoarse. Every once in a while I've paused— so my students can think, I tell them—and concentrated on returning myself to the classroom, *my* classroom, my *real* classroom. But I haven't been able to do it. I guess this world I dreamed is stronger than I am."

"That's why we're here." Conrad put his

hand on Mr. Radagast's weary shoulder. "To help you."

"We'll *all* help you," Damon said, putting his hand on the other shoulder. "Not just Conrad and me, but everyone back in the classroom too."

Mr. Radagast stared straight ahead. A flicker of hope shined in his eyes, but despair swiftly extinguished it. "Oh, if only you could. If only you could."

"How did you think of all this stuff in the first place?" Damon wanted to know.

"It wasn't difficult, once I reasoned how this place works." Mr. Radagast's eyes closed as though the strain had been too much for him. "When I first arrived here, I was absolutely terrified. Obviously, something had gone wrong with the experiment. Instead of the science book, *I* had ceased to exist. Then I realized that this could not be accidental. My students had done this on purpose! They had actually *wanted* me to cease to exist! Can you imagine the horror, the *pain* of that moment?"

Conrad and Damon couldn't look at him or at each other.

"We didn't mean any harm," Conrad said. His throat felt hard, and his voice didn't come out very clear.

"We didn't think it would really work." Damon was having problems with his voice too.

"No, but you hoped it would. And hope was sufficient." Mr. Radagast took a long, shuddering breath. He looked like Damon's Mr. Radagast. But Damon didn't like him this way any more than Conrad did.

"Mr. Radagast, sir, I don't think we have much time." Damon's voice came a little easier as he changed the subject. "We can figure out the rest. You found out how this place works, right? And thought up a perfect classroom, right? And now you want to leave it, right?"

Mr. Radagast nodded assent to all three questions. That should have been the end of it. But Conrad wasn't satisfied.

"Why *do* you want to leave when everything is perfect here?"

"Because it's *boring!*" Mr. Radagast shouted. All at once he looked as angry as when they had come into the classroom. "Absolutely, perfectly *boring!* No one here ever needs extra help, or asks questions, or argues with me, or ignores me. No one ever whispers, or giggles, or carves pictures into the desk tops. There isn't any challenge, or excitement, or intellectual stimulation. It's *boring!* I want to go home!"

"We're *going* home!" Conrad had caught his teacher's revived spirit. "What time is it?"

Mr. Radagast checked his watch. "Six minutes until the end of class."

"Then they'll start thinking us back in sixty seconds, if Louella's watch is right."

"It always is," Damon moaned.

"Let's stand where we would be standing in our classroom, in the front. Maybe that'll make it easier for them."

"Good idea, Conrad." Mr. Radagast snapped to his feet, head held high.

They formed a line—Mr. Radagast in the middle, Conrad to his right, Damon to his left.

Conrad looked out at the empty desks in their ruler-straight rows. Even though he was going to another classroom with ruler-straight rows, he was glad to leave. Friends were waiting for him there, *real* friends, not people he had imagined in his mind. It would be good to be home.

Conrad had a sudden, stabbing thought. "We

still don't know they can think us *into* existence as easily as they thought us away!"

"I have a suggestion," Mr. Radagast said, sounding so much like Louella that, for a moment, Conrad didn't want to go home. "If we concentrate with all our might on returning to the classroom, I submit that our thoughts will merge with the thoughts of the other students and make our passage that much easier."

"It might," Conrad agreed.

"But," said Damon, "we might think up a classroom that looks just like our classroom, but really isn't our classroom. Just like we thought up—" Damon almost said "Mr. Radagast," but Conrad sent him a warning look.

"That could happen, Damon," Mr. Radagast conceded. "But if we wait until we feel our friends' thoughts and *then* join our thoughts with theirs, it should work properly."

"*Will* we feel them?" Conrad asked.

"*I* certainly did," Mr. Radagast said.

"How did they feel?"

"Very strong and hostile." Mr. Radagast shuddered afresh at the memory.

"They won't be hostile this time," Conrad predicted confidently.

Even as he said it, he felt a warm sensation deep inside, a pulling faint and from far away.

"I feel them!" Damon cried.

Mr. Radagast seized their hands and held them tightly. "Close your eyes! Let them take us away! Let our thoughts flow together!"

Conrad closed his eyes. He felt the pulling grow stronger. It spread all over him. With a longing he had never known before, he thought of going back to school, to his classroom, to his desk, to his friends.

Then he tingled all over.

8
Return
to Reality

"They're back!"

"We did it!"

"Hooray!"

Conrad opened his eyes to see his friends
jumping up and down in their seats, clapping
their hands, slapping one another on the back,
and cheering like football fans.

Mr. Radagast let go of Conrad's and Damon's hands. He gazed at the class just like Damon's Mr. Radagast had gazed at his creator. For one awful moment, Conrad was afraid that their teacher was going to break down and cry. But Mr. Radagast pressed his lips tightly together, walked to his desk chair, sat down in it, pulled out his handkerchief, and wiped all traces of emotion from his face. The seventh graders suddenly fell silent.

"Mr. Radagast," Louella said shyly, "are you all right?"

"Sure he's all right," Damon said quickly. "He's just worn out from the—"

BR—R—R—R—RING!

"Class is over!"

"All *right!*"

"Wait until I tell my mom what we did!"

"One moment!"

The students froze by their desks. Their teacher looked weak and weary and even a little mussed, but his voice retained the authority Conrad and Damon had heard in the perfect classroom.

"I would appreciate it," he said calmly, "if you would keep silent about this entire affair, at least for now. We shall discuss it in detail tomorrow. Class dismissed."

All the students except Damon and Conrad nodded, picked up their books, and filed out in perfect order and silence.

When the last one left, Mr. Radagast sighed and said, "A little perfection goes a long, long way."

"We're really back," Conrad said. He couldn't quite believe it.

"We really are," Damon agreed.

"I'm exhausted," Mr. Radagast said, stretching his legs out under his desk.

"So am I."

"Me too. And we still have two more classes to go!"

"No you don't." Mr. Radagast opened his top desk drawer. "I'll write you a pass and excuse you from your classes. It's the least I can do for the people who rescued me."

"Thank you, Mr. Radagast!"

"Thanks a lot!"

He had both passes written in a moment. The delight of a free autumn afternoon banished Conrad's fatigue. But he had a question.

"Why don't you want us to tell anyone what happened?"

Mr. Radagast placed the passes on the edge of the desk. "For one thing, this may have been just a lucky accident, a scientific fluke. I shall have to experiment a little more. On *inanimate* objects. Until I know for sure what we did and how to do it again, until I have total control of the process, I don't want anyone to know what I'm doing. And I certainly don't want word of this—experience—to get into the wrong ears."

"That's for sure," Damon agreed. "People could start disappearing all over the place!"

"Exactly." Mr. Radagast rubbed his brow with the back of his hand. "I only hope I know what I'm doing. I only hope I'm not doing the wrong thing."

"I'm sure you won't be," Conrad said confidently.

"Me too," Damon echoed.

Mr. Radagast smiled. "Run along, boys. Enjoy the afternoon."

Before they left the room, Conrad looked back at Mr. Radagast. He sat serenely in the sunlight, head bowed, eyes closed, hands folded.

"I think he's worrying too much," Conrad said to his friend.

Damon didn't answer. He was staring straight ahead.

Conrad looked up the hall in time to see Louella turn the corner.

"Damon!"

"Just daydreaming, Conrad."

"We *promised.*"

"We promised not to *talk* about it. He didn't say a word about *experimenting* with it. See you tomorrow, hero boy."

Damon ducked into the boys' rest room, whistling as he went, leaving Conrad to wonder if Mr. Radagast was worrying *enough.*

But it had taken the entire class to think one person away. Surely, one mind wasn't strong enough to do any damage.

All the same, he was glad to see Louella go safely into her next classroom.

And *that* was something he had *never* expected to feel.